Susan King loved her job as a school teacher. Having been raised in the small Amish *Ordnung* of Shipshewana, she'd been around both Amish and *Englischers* most of her life. When the time had come for her to choose her path, the decision had been an easy one for her.

She loved children and helping them choose the right path came naturally to her. She was so grateful that the Amish school had given her a chance to share her love of *Gott, familye,* and the Amish way of life. She counted her day a success when one of her pupils finally grasped a new concept, or mastered the knowledge of a basic skill. Watching her young chargers learn to read and write was very fulfilling for her and she thanked *Gott* on a daily basis for allowing her to have such enjoyable work.

Her pupils seemed to enjoy her being there teacher as well. They seldom left her classroom with frowns upon their faces; rather, smiles and childish laughter seemed to abound in *Fraulein* King's classes. Their parents were always sending their *kinner* to school with a basket of bread, pickings from their gardens, or fabric to be used for one project or another. She felt very needed.

This particular spring day, she was happy to see her pupils leave the small school house and head for their homes. It had been an unusually warm day for April, and the children had been restless and unfocused as they dreamt of spending some time in the sunshine. Winter was finally gone and the promise of summer was very tempting to her young charges.

Susan understood their desires, having the same ones herself. She'd found it impossible to reprimand them for their inattention, finding her own eyes straying to the sunshine and blue skies just outside the schoolroom windows. She loved working outdoors when the weather was starting to warm up and even though the arrival of summer meant more chores, she didn't care. As a single woman, she still lived with her *daed* and *mamm*. As the youngest of six children, she had been given the privilege of finding work away from the farm. Her older siblings were all married and raising *kinner* of their own. She was often called to babysit her nieces and nephews, but farm chores were mostly covered by others.

That left plenty of room for Susan to do what she loved. Work with *kinner* as a teacher!

She walked around the small room, straightening chairs, picking up items that had been put away in the wrong place, and then she swept the wooden floorboards clean. She'd adopted the habit of setting the room to rights after each session, knowing that other people would be utilizing the room before she arrived next.

She currently taught the nine and ten-year old *kinner*, while other's taught the other age groups. They currently went to school in the mornings Tuesday thru Friday, leaving plenty of time for other activities and to help their *familyes* in the afternoons and on the weekends.

She surveyed the small room one last time and then retrieved her lunch pail and the small satchel she used to contain her school materials. As she reached for the handle, she was alarmed to hear a ripping sound and then feel the bag slip from her hands as it landed on the floorboards with a loud thud.

She looked down and saw that the leather strap had broken clean through. The satchel was one that had been used for many years by others, but Susan hadn't minded when it was given to her at all. It had a long enough strap that she could slip it over her shoulder and allow it to drape crosswise over her body, making carrying it as she walked to and from the school house and easy chore.

She picked up the broken strap, carefully analyzing it to see if it was repairable, and then shook her head. It was not. The years of wear had weakened the leather to the point that it could no longer handle the weight and stress associated with carrying the bag's contents.

With a soft sigh, she carefully undid the strap and then laid the bag and her books on the closest desk. The town was only a few short blocks away and she knew she would be able to find something there that would serve the purpose the leather bag had been doing.

"I'll just come back for my books on the way home this afternoon."

She tucked some money into the pocket of her apron, along with the key for the school house and stepped outside. It was going on one o'clock in the afternoon, and she tipped her head back and allowed the sun to shine fully on her face for a few brief moments. It felt wonderful and brought a smile to her face.

She was still smiling as she started walking towards the small town. Shipshewana was a complex town where the Amish lifestyle was readily combined with *Englisch* commerce and social atmosphere. Many of the Amish sold their wares in the shops along the two main streets, attracting not only other Amish, but a large number of tourists from the surrounding cities.

Everything from Amish buggies, to cured meats and cheeses, could be purchased in the small shops, and Susan was sure she would be able to find a replacement for the bag in one of the shops. Even if it was in an *Englisch* shop.

With that goal in mind, she finished her walk quickly and began to wander down the sidewalk in search of the perfect book bag. She'd not been to the town in a number of months, and she was amazed to see a variety of new stores had opened up. It seemed the *Englisch* were thriving here and she knew it had to be due in part to their Amish counterparts.

She wandered down the main street, but when she reached the end, she was no closer to finding a bag, than when she'd began her search. She walked along the cross street, eyeing the large building that had been erected up ahead and wondering what kind of business was conducted there. Deciding there was no harm in looking, she walked towards it and stopped in front of the wooden sign.

Forrester Children's Home.

She read the sign several times before she realized it was advertising an orphanage. She'd heard her *daed* and *mamm* talking several months back about the *Englisch* and how they dealt with their parentless *kinner*. Rather than finding other *familye* members to take in the *kinner* and raise them, they placed them together in a dormitory style *haus* and then kept them there until a suitable *haus* could be found for them with strangers.

Susan had thought at the time how sad that was for the *kinner*, but her *daed* had gone on to say it was how the *Englisch* did things. The Amish would never consider placing *kinner* in a situation like that. Allowing the government to have any say in how or where their *kinner* were raised would never be allowed. Never.

She was still standing there pondering the differences between the Amish and *Englisch*, when she felt a presence to her left side. She turned and saw a very handsome young man watching her.

"Hi," she offered, along with a soft smile. Susan was always kind, even to her own detriment at times.

"Hello. What are you doing?" he asked with a pleasant voice.

"I was in the town and saw this building had recently been erected. I wanted to know what kind of business operated inside it."

The young man nodded his head, "Sounds reasonable, but not a business."

Susan smiled in return, "I see that." She looked at him and then asked, "Are you going inside?"

"Yes. I volunteer here several times a week. Want to come inside with me and look around?"

The offer was very tempting and Susan found herself accepting it without a second thought. "I would like that."

"Very well, follow me. I'm Ralph, by the way."

She nodded at him, "I'm Susan."

"You're Amish?" he questioned, taking in her attire as they walked up the concrete path that led towards the front doors.

"*Ja.* What was your first clue?" She waited for him to comment on her attire, her prayer *kapp*, or even the fact that she was obviously travelling on foot, but he did none of the above.

Ralph looked her up and down and then lowered his voice, "Your smile."

Susan wasn't prepared for that answer and looked at him for a moment before she realized he was flirting with her. She blushed and ducked her eyes as he opened the door for her to pass through first. "Ladies first."

"*Danke.*" She stepped inside the foyer, biting the inside of her cheek as her eyes moved around the room, taking it all in. The room contained white tile floors and white walls, with very modern looking chairs set against it in a light green color. Pictures of children adorned the walls, but rather than smiling faces, most of the children looked lost and sad. It broke Susan's heart to see them so.

"Who are those children?"

Ralph studied the pictures with her, "Those are pictures of some of the children who have come through the orphanage here. Many of them are victims of tragedies where their parents have been killed, and a few of them were abandoned at birth. They come here, rather than going into the state foster care system so that they can be adopted out sooner rather than later."

"Why don't you come meet some of the children?" Ralph suggested, watching the expressions move over Susan's face. She was a beautiful girl, with a creamy smooth complexion devoid of makeup. Her hair was pulled back from her face and covered by the white mesh material all of the Amish wore.

She had the customary plain dress on, in a cornflower blue, with no buttons or zippers, or other forms of adornment. He knew from asking questions over the years, that the Amish avoided any outward adornments that might serve to make them prideful in their appearance. They didn't have mirrors in their homes, and jewelry was taboo.

"Would that be allowed?" Susan asked quietly, the light of interest in her eyes something he found he might like to see more of.

"Sure. Follow me," Ralph preceded her down the long hallway. Just before they reached the classroom where he was scheduled to work this afternoon, The house mother, Mrs. Templeton met up with them.

"Ralph, you've brought along a friend today?"

Ralph shook his head, "No…well, not yet anyway." He slid a glance Susan's way and then explained her presence to Mrs. Templeton. "This is Susan and she was standing in front of the sign when I arrived. I was going to show her some of the children the orphanage helps take care of."

Mrs. Templeton looked at Susan and smiled, "Susan, welcome."

Susan inclined her head, asking softly, "Are there many children living here?"

Mrs. Templeton nodded her head sadly, "I'm afraid there is. We are at capacity, and have two more children arriving later this afternoon."

"Capacity?" Susan queried.

"Yes, we currently have beds for thirty-two children ranging in ages from infant up through when they turn sixteen or finish high school. We don't currently have any children over the age of five in residence, but that can always change."

Susan narrowed her brow, "This building looks like it could house many more children than thirty-two."

Mrs. Templeton nodded at her observation, "That is true, however, I cannot abide the thought of these children simply wasting away here while they wait for a more permanent place to go. We offer them education, play time, and positive social interactions with both adults and other children. Since implementing that program several years ago, they seem to be much happier and easier to place with forever families."

Ralph interjected, "But the programs she's talking about require a lot of volunteers. I love it here, but it's hard to find people who will commit to a regular schedule."

Susan nodded, looking thoughtful once more. "Could I wander around for a bit?"

Mrs. Templeton nodded her head, "Yes. Ralph, story time isn't set to begin for another twenty minutes or so. Feel free to show your new friend around."

Ralph nodded and then led the way to where the children were playing or being cared for. Susan was pleased to see that every room had a viewing window, located so that adults could look in, but the children inside wouldn't be distracted by being observed.

Their first stop was a sort of nursery, with playpens and blankets scattered around the room, with infants just learning to roll over, or sit up, occupying space in each one. Three women walked amongst them, checking on diapers and talking to the little ones. They didn't miss an opportunity to give them a loving hug or familiar touch.

The next rooms held *kinner* of various ages, all of them playing in a groups of two or three, while at least one adult looked on or directed the play. They were much younger than the *kinner* she was used to spending time with, and she briefly wondered why the orphanage was having trouble finding volunteers. The *kinner* seemed happy, and the work easy.

As they finished their tour, an idea came to her and she bid Ralph goodbye and went in search of Mrs. Templeton. She had a sudden desire to volunteer a few hours each week to help make life a little better for these unfortunate *kinner.*

When she walked out of the orphanage half an hour later, she was smiling to herself, and glad that she'd made the trip into the small town. She headed home, a lightness to her steps as she thought about her first day at the orphanage. It wouldn't occur for another week, giving her a chance to exercise patience mixed with a healthy dose of anticipation.

Eight days later, Saturday...

Susan arrived at the orphanage right on time the following Saturday and dutifully filled out the paperwork Mrs. Templeton had waiting for her.

"These forms are just a formality, you understand?" she made sure Susan was aware that the forms didn't obligate her to do anything. Susan appreciated the woman's explanation, and hoped she would never have to explain the forms to her *daed* and *mamm.*

She'd not told anyone in the *Ordnung* that she was going to be volunteering in an *Englisch* orphanage for a variety of reasons. First, no one had asked. Second, she knew if she offered the information, she would have to answer many questions and hear the notes of disapproval in their voices. The Amish believed in taking care of their own, and letting others do the same. Her parents would be anything but happy to find her trying to make life a little better for the *Englisch kinner.*

Pushing those unpleasant thoughts aside, she followed Mrs. Templeton down the hallway, only to find herself being ushered into the five-year old arts and crafts room. Eight children were being supervised there, and when Mrs. Templeton had made the proper introductions, both of the other women quickly disappeared.

Susan watched as the other women left and then turned to see all of the *kinner* watching her warily. She gave them a tentative smile and then slowly made her way to the small table where they were all coloring on blank paper.

"Good morning," she told them, looking around the table and meeting each of their eyes. They soon went back to their artwork and she sat quietly, watching them draw and color. When one of the little girls grew tired of coloring, she crawled into Susan's lap, popped her thumb into her mouth, and laid her head on her chest.

Susan hugged the little body close to her, only to feel her heart soften when several of the other *kinner* followed suit. Within a few minutes, she was surrounded by warm little bodies, all wanting some personal contact with her. She quickly made a decision that a trip to the outdoor playground was needed to help get their little minds onto something besides how lonely they were.

"How would you all like to go outside and swing?" she asked, glancing around at the sixteen eyes that watched her. "Does that not sound like fun? The sun is shining."

She lifted the little girl, who tag on the back of her t-shirt identified her name as Amber, to the tiled floor and stood up carefully, not wanting to topple any of the *kinner* still leaning against her legs to the ground.

Amber immediately reached for her hand and she smiled warmly down at the little one. "Come *kinner,* let's go play." She led the way towards the exit door at the rear of the room, pushed it open and then waited while they all filed out after her. Another group of smaller *kinner* was playing outside as well, and she urged her small charges to go and join them.

She pushed each one on the swings, and once they were all playing, she located a bench under a nearby tree and sat down to observe them. They had so much energy, something she'd not prepared herself for. She'd also not expected the playing outside would only serve to make them hyper.

The younger group headed back indoors, and ten minutes later she rounded up her small charges and herded them back to the classroom, her mind spinning furiously as she tried to come up with a new plan. She'd brought along some paper crafts, but they were filled with too much energy to sit quietly for such an activity.

"Why don't we all have a seat on the carpet over there?" she suggested, spying the color carpet on the floor in the corner of the room. She joined them, lowering herself to a low stool and watching as they all sat down around her feet. "Do you like music?" she asked, watching as some of them nodded.

"How about I teach you a song I learned as a young girl?"

"Did your mommy sing it to you?" Amber wanted to know.

Susan smiled at her questioned and answered her, "*Ja*. My *mamm* sang it to me when I was your age."

Amber's response was not what she expected. The little girl looked said and then murmured, "I don't have a mommy." Her thumb found her mouth again and she sat there looking forlorn as she sucked on it.

Tears sprang to Susan's eyes and it was only by sheer force of will that she was able to sing the simple song and teach it to the *kinner*. Her compassionate heart broke for the little ones currently in her care, for their heartache, and the fact that for one reason or another they had been left homeless and parentless. It made her even more cognizant of how lucky she and her siblings had been.

Danke, Gott! If I've ever been ungrateful for my daed and mamm, please forgive me. Danke for giving me such loving examples of Your love in them. And please send loving familyes for these kinner, that they might also know the security and love that comes with being part of a familye.

"Susan?" a male voice called from behind her. She turned around to see Ralph standing at the door with a quizzical look upon his face.

"Hello," she replied with a smile.

"What are you doing here?" he asked, stepping further into the room.

Before she could answer him, Peter captured her attention by standing on one of the tables. "Peter, standing on the tables is not allowed. Would you please step down?"

Peter gave her a frown, but when she held his gaze, he reluctantly did as she'd asked. She smiled at him, "*Danke.*" When the young boy just stood there, watching her, she waved her hand towards the others, "Go play."

He did so, looking back at her several times, as if he expected her to come after him. Susan was confused and it must have shown on her face.

Ralph stepped up beside her, "You're good with them." When she raised a brow in his direction he went on, "Peter has only been here a few weeks. He was in a foster home, but they abused him. He's a little wary around the adults here."

Susan looked back at the little boy, sending up a silent prayer that his next home would be full of love and kindness. When a yawn caught her unawares, she covered her mouth with her hand and blushed bright red.

Ralph chuckled, "Tired?"

Susan finished her yawn and then nodded, "I'm not used to being around *kinner* with so much energy."

"*Kinner?* Is that Amish for kids?" Ralph asked with a grin.

Susan looked at him, "Children. *Kinner* means children. Kids are baby goats." She said it with a straight face, smiling when Ralph realized she'd been attempting humor.

"Good one. So…you decided to volunteer?"

"*Ja*. I can only come on Saturday's, but Mrs. Templeton said that was perfect because many people don't want to give up their weekends to spend time here."

"That's true," Ralph agreed with a nod. "Most people want to enjoy their days off. Which brings me to the question … why don't you want to enjoy your weekends doing…whatever it is that the Amish do for fun?"

Susan laughed softly at the expression on his face. It was obvious that Ralph didn't really know much about their lifestyle and she took the time to explain how they lived to him. "The Amish live a very simple lifestyle. For us, gathering with our *familye* or other members of the *Ordnung* is fun. There is always work to be done, and while there are down times, there are always a variety of other chores that need to be done then."

"That sounds kind of boring…"

"Maybe, but there is great satisfaction in planting seeds, watching them grow, and then harvesting the fruit of one's labor several months later."

Ralph shrugged his shoulders, "I guess, I've never grown anything. I've lived in cities all of my life. Someone gave me a plant once, but I forgot to water it for a couple of weeks and it turned brown and died."

Susan tried to hide her smile, but in the end, she couldn't contain a small chuckle. "Plants like water…"

"Yeah, I figured that out."

Susan started to respond, but Amber tugged on her hand, gesturing for her to lean down so she could whisper in her ear. Hearing the little girl's request to use the bathroom had Susan blinking and then quickly looking to Ralph for his assistance. She'd been so excited to meet the *kinner*, she'd forgotten to ask where the bathroom was located.

Ralph quickly ascertained what was needed and pointed her towards the other end of the room where a closed door stood sentry. "Each room has their own."

Susan nodded and escorted the little girl towards the bathroom, murmuring over her shoulder, "*Danke.*"

"I'm going to assume that means 'thanks'. See you around Susan." Ralph gave her a smile and then headed out of the classroom.

She watched him leave for a moment, but the urgent tugging on her hand required immediate attention. She smiled at the little girl and opened the door, "There you go. Can you manage on your own?" she asked, relieved when Amber nodded her head. This was yet another reminder that she was slightly out of her comfort zone with *kinner* this young.

And yet, as her volunteer time came to a close, she left the orphanage excited about returning the next week. And not only to see the *kinner*. There was something about Ralph that drew her to him and she had to remind herself that he was *Englisch*. That fact alone should have caused her to push him out of her mind, and yet she found herself thinking about him throughout the week more and more.

Three weeks later, Saturday at the orphanage…

Susan tossed the ball towards Peter, clapping along with the others when he hit the ball with the plastic bat and took off running. Ralph had explained the game to her, calling it a slightly modified version of baseball, with a plastic bat and a beach ball for the target.

The *kinner* screamed in glee as Ralph caught the ball and ran after Peter. He intentionally made himself stumble, allowing the little boy a chance to run around the bases and reach home before he could be tagged.

Ralph pretended to be upset that he'd missed an opportunity, but Susan could tell he was enjoying watching their celebration. "That was kind of you," she told him a few minutes later when Mrs. Templeton appeared with two other volunteers and a bucket of ice cream and box of cones.

"Was it?" he asked her with a slight smirk.

"You could have easily tagged him with the ball."

"But where would the fun have been in that?" he asked, reaching for her hand and pulling her along towards where the ice cream was being delved out.

Susan extricated her hand as quickly as possible, rubbing her palm along her skirts to get rid of the tingles his touch had created. "Ice cream sounds like a pleasant treat for the *kinner*."

"They deserve some treats now and then. My great grandfather loved doing things that brought smiles to their faces."

"Your great grandfather?" she asked, taking the proffered cone from one of the other volunteers.

Ralph took his own cone and nodded as they walked towards a vacant bench, "My great grandfather founded this orphanage. I always make a point of coming here and volunteering when I'm on vacation from the university."

Susan nodded, cataloging that piece of information in her brain. Before she could think up a reply, Amber and Peter both joined them, "Miss Susan, sing us the song about the snake."

She smiled at them, the request one she received each time she visited. On her second day of volunteering, she'd taught the *kinner* some simple songs, but their favorite had been about a snake that had envisioned himself a bird. Now they wanted to hear it constantly.

Susan smiled down at them, "Only if you both sing it with me." Two eager heads nodded and she softly began to sing about the poor snake, tired of slithering along the ground in the mud, who decided he wished to be a bird.

He taught himself how to climb the tallest tree he could find, but then couldn't get down. Now on the land, he'd been swift and the birds had been wary of him. But in the tree, one of them decided to befriend him.

After talking with the bird about his predicament, the bird offered his help, but instead of carrying the snake back down to the ground, the bird carried him away, ending the snakes story as he became lunch for the bird.

Ralph listened to the song and then asked, "Not a very happy ending."

Susan nodded her head as the two little ones scampered off to play with the other *kinner*, "Not all stories have happy endings. Sometimes they simply have a moral the listeners are supposed to heed." She paused and then explained, "The snake was unhappy with his lot in life and envied being something else. That action caused him his life in the end."

"So the moral is that he should have been content and happy where he was, and he would have lived a long life."

"Exactly," she told him with a smile.

"You're really good with them. So, exactly how old are you?"

Susan looked at him and then offered, "Twenty-two. How old are you?"

"Twenty-four. I just graduated from the university and just have to decide if I want to continue, or get a job."

"Continue?"

"With graduate school. Frankly, the idea of being a student for another four to six years doesn't appeal to me at all."

"That seems like a long time," she agreed. She started to ask him what his degree was in, but the arrival of a new person kept her silent. The woman was tall, thin, and gorgeous. She walked across the lawn, came directly up to Ralph and wrapped her arms around his shoulders. Susan looked on in shock when she kissed him on the lips, in full view of everyone.

"Hey, baby," she murmured as she stepped back and smoothed her manicured hands down her short skirt.

"Rachel! This is a surprise," Ralph told her with a smile. "What are you doing here?"

"I came by to see you, silly." Rachel glanced over at Susan, looking down her nose at her, and then dismissing her quickly. "Who's that?" she whispered loudly enough that Susan could hear.

Ralph turned his head and then smiled at Susan, "Susan, this is my girlfriend Rachel. This is Susan, she volunteers here on Saturdays."

"Great!" Rachel gave her a quick scathing look and then turned her back on her.

Susan tried not to let the girl's attitude bother her, after all, she was his girlfriend. *What was I thinking?* She'd had thoughts of Ralph in her mind for weeks now, but he'd never mentioned a girlfriend and she knew she only had herself to blame for thinking the two of them ever had any possibility of becoming something more than acquaintances.

Ralph made her laugh, and over the last few weeks, they'd spent more and more time together at the orphanage. She'd begun to think of ways around the fact that he was *Englisch*, knowing full well her *mamm* and *daed* would be disappointed in her thoughts and actions. They still didn't know that she was volunteering at the orphanage, and she'd decided to keep it that way a while longer.

They were always worried that people were going to take advantage of her, and they had an irrational...almost hatred, towards the *Englischers*. Susan was sure it was created by their fear of the unknown, but nevertheless, she didn't want them trying to dissuade her from volunteering at the orphanage, so she kept her whereabouts quiet. She knew if they would just take the time to get to know some of the *Englishcers*, they would feel differently, but she wasn't prepared to be the one to suggest that to them.

"...almost ready? This place gives me the creeps. I'm ready to get out of here."

Ralph glanced at Susan, who ducked her head to hide the fact that her face felt slightly warm with embarrassment. Rachel was tracing one of her red painted fingernails over his chest, and standing so close to him, Susan was sure they were touching in multiple places.

"I was going to stick around for another hour or so..."

Rachel pouted prettily, "An hour? That's much too long." She looked at Susan and addressed her, "You don't mind taking over whatever he was doing, do you?"

Susan shook her head, "Uhm...well, the *kinner* are staying together today, so I guess it wouldn't hurt if you left earlier than intended." She said the last to Ralph, having a hard time meeting his eyes.

He was so handsome and nice, and is big heart was evident every time she saw him. *Of course he has a girlfriend, silly. He's quite the catch. Any girl would be lucky to have a relationship with him.*

"Are you sure, Susan?" he asked her.

"Of course she's sure," Rachel answered for her. "Go grab your things so we can get out of here."

Susan nodded weakly at Ralph and he thanked her and then jogged towards the building. Susan turned to say something to his girlfriend, but gone was the semi-pleasant woman of a few moments ago. Now she only gave her an icy stare that made Susan want to be anywhere but standing there next to her.

Ralph returned moments later and bid her farewell, "See you next week?"

"Sure. I'll be here," she told him with a smile. Rachel glared at her so that Ralph couldn't see, and Susan's smile fell away. She'd done nothing deserving of the woman's attitude, but it was plain to see that Rachel did not like Susan for one reason or another.

"Did Ralph leave?" Mrs. Templeton asked, coming up on her right side.

"*Ja.* His girlfriend showed up."

"Ah. Let me guess, Rachel Dunn?"

Susan nodded, "She seems rather unhappy."

"She's shallow and vain, and frankly, not a very nice person. She doesn't usually show up here, she's afraid one of the kids might get her clothes dirty or something like that."

Susan smiled, looking down at her own apron, stained with the remains of a finger painting craft they'd done together earlier that morning. "She'd be right about that."

Mrs. Templeton saw where her eyes were and chuckled, "Hope that paint comes out."

Susan nodded, "It will, or it will become my permanent craft apron." She pasted a smile back on her face, "What's next for the afternoon?"

"A walk to pick flowers. Can you handle supervising half of Ralph's if I give the other half to Amy?"

"Of course. Picking flowers sounds like a fun activity."

Mrs. Templeton laughed, "We'll see how many flowers actually make it back intact. The last time we did this, the grasses were taller than some of the kids and we ended up playing hide and seek with them for hours."

Susan raised her brow and then a thought came to her, "Do you still have some of those candies you gave the *kinner* last week?"

"The chocolate ones?"

Susan nodded, "*Ja.* How about if we have the *kinner* find us? Each time they check in, they get a candy for their efforts."

Mrs. Templeton nodded her head, "I hadn't thought of that, but it just might work. They sure do like candy. Let me grab the bag from my office and then we'll head out." She wandered off and Susan found herself trying to place a nice boy like Ralph, with a girl like Rachel. It was hard to do, and yet she'd seen it with her own eyes.

This is why you need to stop thinking about him. He's not only Englisch, but he's taken. He's not for you!

Beginning of July...

Susan finished braiding Amber's hair and then looked up as the door to the community classroom opened. She tried to school her features when she saw Rachel standing there, scanning the room for Ralph. The woman was beautiful on the outside, but Susan had felt the ugliness she hid inside more than once and had no desire to ruin the day by dealing with her.

She glanced towards the window to the activity room, and was disappointed to see that Ralph wasn't back yet. Mrs. Templeton had sent him into town to run and errand, which meant Rachel was going to be looking for someone to deal with her. *I hope that person doesn't become me.* She immediately felt bad for thinking that way; she was normally kind to everyone and she mentally lectured herself to change her attitude.

When Rachel headed her way, Susan forced herself to remain seated at the small table. "Where is he?" Rachel demanded to know when she was but a few feet away.

Susan mentally took a deep breath and then calmly answered, "He's running an errand for Mrs. Templeton."

"And who is Mrs. Templeton?" Rachel asked, sarcasm and dislike for being at the orphanage dripping from her tone of voice.

"The woman who runs the orphanage. He should be back in a few minutes." Susan was trying to be civil, but Rachel made that very challenging. Since the first time she'd met Rachel, and Rachel had met her, the woman had been dropping by the orphanage on Saturday's more frequently. She never missed an opportunity to make sure Susan knew she was there because Ralph was her boyfriend, and that he was all hers. It was as if she felt threatened by Susan, which was a ridiculous notion.

Rachel never bothered to tell Ralph when she was going to be stopping by, and more than once she'd pouted and Ralph had felt forced to leave early. During those times, the extra work usually fell to Susan, and she tried not to mind.

The few times Susan had tried to engage the woman in conversation, Rachel had not been very receptive, so Susan had started keeping her distance. It wasn't a hardship because she wasn't sure she even liked the woman. A fact that had caused her more than a few conversations with *Gott.*

Susan knew she was supposed to show *Gott's* love to everyone, but people like Rachel made that very difficult. "Would you like to sit down and wait for him?" she asked, gesturing towards an empty chair at the table.

"In here? With all of these kids? I don't think so," Rachel told her, looking at the *kinner* like they were contaminated or something. Her attitude bothered Susan and she found herself wondering once again what Ralph saw in her. He loved working with the *kinner* and it was an easy stretch of her imagination to see him playing *daed* in the near future.

She was still pondering that question when she saw a movement in the adjoining room. Ralph had returned and Rachel removed herself from the room, allowing Susan to breathe easier once again. She finished her shift and then headed back to the *familye haus.* Her parents hadn't yet asked what she was doing every Saturday morning, and she'd not volunteered that information. Today had been the closest they had come to asking. Her mother had begun to harvest some of the vegetables from the garden, and her two *schwestern* were spending the day at their childhood h*aus*, canning and preparing the Earth's bounty. And Susan was expected to help.

"Susan, your *schwestern* will be arriving shortly after lunch. Will you be here at that time?" her *mamm* had asked her that morning at breakfast.

"Not until after one o'clock," Susan had answered. She'd been spending more time at the orphanage, especially on those days when Ralph worked the afternoon shift. She enjoyed being around him, and even though she didn't see any redeeming qualities in Rachel, she didn't fault Ralph for being with her.

Sensing her *mamm* watching her carefully, she'd smiled and promised her *mamm* that she would be home by early afternoon. She'd let Mrs. Templeton know she would be leaving early as soon as she'd arrived today. The older woman had smiled and happily agreed to cover for her until the night volunteers arrived, telling her she thought it was nice that she knew how to can vegetables and such.

Glancing at the clock, she saw it was almost time to leave. She gathered up the construction paper she'd been cutting into strips and place everything on the table back into the plastic basket. Mrs. Templeton would help the older *kinner* make the rainbow chain this afternoon while the younger ones took a nap.

Once she'd checked that Mrs. Templeton was still okay if she left early, she exchanged her paint stained apron for the clean one she'd arrived in and headed for the front doors. She stepped outside, frowning when she saw the thunderclouds gathering overhead. Summer rain storms were frequent this time of year, and she hurried down the steps, hoping to make it most of the way home before the clouds released the rain they carried.

She ducked her head when the wind picked up and the first raindrops started to fall, hurrying as fast as she could without running and possibly slipping in the quickly forming mud. The honking of a horn startled her a few seconds later, and she skidded to a stop, looking up to see Rachel driving past her with Ralph in the passenger seat.

He had the window rolled down and after exchanging a few harsh words with Rachel, she stopped the vehicle and waited for Susan to come even with his window.

"Susan, what are you doing walking in this rain?" Ralph asked incredulously.

Susan smiled at him, the rain starting to soak through her dress and making her shiver. "I walk everywhere unless with a member of my *familye* in their buggy. I'll be fine."

"Get in. We'll give you a ride home," Ralph offered, opening his door despite Rachel protesting.

Susan stepped back and shook her head, another shiver reminding her she still had a two mile walk as the crow flies. "*Nee.* I'll be fine. I need to go." She skirted around the front of the vehicle and quickly crossed the street, heading for the small path that led through the woods to her *daed's* farm. Using the established roads, she would be looking at a five mile walk, but the dirt paths crossed Amish land, and if she hurried, she would be home in about twenty minutes.

She didn't look back to see if Ralph and Rachel were still watching her, she didn't want to know. Ralph was a nice man, despite being *Englisch*, and if he didn't have a girlfriend, Susan might feel justified daydreaming about him in a romantic fashion. But that wasn't the case, and she'd been taught from an early age that coveting something, or someone, that was already spoken for was a sin.

Ralph was taken, and while Susan didn't think he deserved someone like Rachel, she had to admit that he was an adult and capable of making his own decisions. But turning off her feelings about him, was getting harder each week. She'd even found herself comparing him with the single Amish *menner* she saw from time to time.

She stepped out of the woods, soaked to the skin as the rain steadily increased, and she hurried towards the *haus* in the distance. She pushed thoughts of the orphanage, Ralph, and Rachel to the back of her mind, thinking instead of the work to be done yet this day. Hard work would keep her mind occupied and keep her from thinking about things she shouldn't.

Four weeks later…

Ralph watched Rachel step out of the orphanage's patio door and mentally groaned. No matter how many times he'd assured her there was nothing going on between himself and the *little Amish girl*, Rachel still felt the need to check up on him when she knew Susan would be around.

He liked Susan. She was kind, compassionate, and unlike Rachel, she made it a habit of never speaking ill about others. Unlike himself. In fact, when he thought about Susan, she made him very aware of his shortcomings.

Susan always put others above herself, and Ralph wondered what her life must really be like. He knew she lived with her parents, and that they used no electricity, nor did they drive automobiles. He personally couldn't imagine doing without his cell phone and other modern conveniences, and yet Susan seemed very happy without them.

Rachel hadn't seen him yet, and he took a moment to observe her as she approached Susan. He saw Susan's shoulder's tighten up in anticipation of dealing with Rachel's demands, but the smile on her face never faltered.

Deciding Susan didn't deserve the third degree he knew Rachel was going to subject her to, he headed in their direction. Rachel didn't understand Susan, and when Ralph had dared to suggest that maybe she could befriend the Amish girl, Rachel had simply scoffed at him and called him crazy.

That was why he was so shocked to hear Rachel talking sweetly to her as he came up behind them.

"So, you really should come, it's going to be a cool party," Rachel was saying.

Ralph frowned and stepped between them, "What's going to be a cool party?"

Rachel turned her head and smiled at him, "My birthday party, silly. Don't you remember? I think it would be so cool if Susan could join us, don't you?"

Ralph looked at Rachel for a moment, but she seemed sincere and he was willing to give her the benefit of the doubt. Addressing Susan, he nodded his head, "Rachel's right. You should definitely come to the party."

Susan shook her head, "I appreciate you inviting me, but I could never come to an *Englisch* party."

"Why not? We don't bite," Ralph teased her.

Susan smiled and blushed, "I know you don't bite, but I really couldn't…"

"Don't you want to?" Rachel asked with a convincing pout that Ralph knew meant she was preparing to do battle. Rachel didn't like being told "No" and refusing and invitation from her was almost the same in her mind.

Susan smiled at Rachel, "I actually would love to attend your birthday party, but I don't have anything to wear. All of my dresses are just like this one, and I wouldn't want to embarrass you in front of your friends."

Ralph thought it cute how Susan was afraid she might embarrass Rachel, but he held his tongue when Rachel spoke again.

"Don't worry about that. I have the perfect dress in my closet that you can borrow."

"Really? You would loan me a dress to wear?" Susan asked.

"Sure."

Ralph was shocked at how nice Rachel was being and secretly hoped that maybe spending some time with Susan would be a good thing for her. "Susan, you need to come. It's Wednesday evening."

Rachel nodded, "At 8 o'clock." She pulled a piece of paper from her purse and jotted down her address, "Just come to this address. It's only a few blocks from here."

Susan took the piece of paper and Ralph watched her tuck it carefully into the pocket of her dress. Rachel was being nice to Susan, for the first time, and Ralph found himself feeling proud of her.

After Susan took herself back inside the orphanage, he pulled Rachel close and kissed her, "Thank you for inviting her."

Rachel shrugged and then slipped an arm around his waist, "She seems like a nice girl. Why not let her see what's she missing?"

Ralph grinned, "I knew you would like her if you just gave her a chance."

Rachel just gave him a small smile and then turned and walked with him towards the exit, "I'll see you a little later. I have a few errands to run."

Ralph raised a brow at her and asked, "Do you want me to come with you? I was planning on leaving in half an hour anyway?"

For the first time, she seemed content to have me stick around the orphanage a bit longer. She shook her head, "No, you stay and finish your shift. I'll see you at dinner tonight." She gave him a quick kiss and then waved her fingers as she took her leave. Ralph watched her for a moment, amazed at the apparent transformation in her. But not amazed enough to rock the boat and ask her what had precipitated this attitude change. *I'm just going to enjoy it for however long it lasts.*

*****

Susan finished her volunteer shift, anxious to leave and find a few moments along to contemplate the strange invitation Rachel had given her. The girl had acted friendly towards her, even going so far as to offer to loan her a dress so she wouldn't stick out at the party.

Susan longed to experience an *Englisch* party. During her *Rumspringa*, she'd not had the opportunity to attend anything but a few tame parties where foul smelling beer had been present. The attendees had mostly been other Amish, all looking to explore whether they truly wanted to live the Amish lifestyle as adults. The parties had been dull and a disappointment.

But something told her Rachel would never throw a tame party and Susan found herself looking forward to Wednesday more than she ought. It just happened to coincide with a four day weekend, so she would be able to attend the party and not have to worry about being tired the next morning.

She struggled to contain her growing excitement over the next four days, throwing herself into her work at the school, and at the *familye* farm. It was the beginning of harvest season, so finding extra chores to do wasn't hard, and everyone was worn out by the end of the day.

Wednesday was no different. The *kinner* had held classes only in the morning, going to their individual farms to lend extra hands wherever needed. Susan had spent the afternoon peeling peaches and turning them into preserves, jams and jellies to be sold at the store in town. The *Engllschers* never seemed to tire of purchasing Amish-made goods, these included food items and things like furniture and quilts.

After helping her *mamm* clean up the kitchen, she bid both of her parents a goodnight and headed off to her bedroom at the back of the *haus*. She sat on her bed, her heart racing as she waited to hear her *daed's* heavy footsteps climb the stairs for bed. Tonight was Rachel's party, and even though she knew her parents would be terribly disappointed in her if they were to ever find out what she was about to do, she so longed to experience the social life of the *Englisch*. Just once.

A few minutes after 8 o'clock, the *haus* finally grew quiet and she knew it was now or never. She slipped out of her bedroom door, grateful that she'd just oiled the hinges a few weeks earlier, and opened the backdoor. She pushed herself to walk quickly through the darkened path that led back into town, hoping she wasn't going to be too late to the party. Rachel had told her to come when she was able, she only hoped she wasn't making a huge mistake.

She felt guilty for the thoughts that ran through her mind, but a part of her was hoping that if Ralph could see her in his world, he might realize he didn't have to stay with someone like Rachel. That she could fit into his world. She'd never thought of leaving the Amish lifestyle she'd been born into, and yet…the allure of the *Englisch* had always been there. Bidding her to step away from all that she knows and try something new.

What harm could come from just testing the waters a bit?

Susan arrived at the address Rachel had given her and slowly made her way to the front door. Loud music came from inside, and a number of vehicles were parked in the driveway and up and down the street. It appeared the party was well under way and she was hoping she wasn't too late.

She knocked on the door and then gasped when it was pulled open and Ralph greeted her with a big smile.

"Susan! You came!" He reached out and pulled inside the doorway by the arm. Susan tried to ignore the tingles that raced up her arm where he touched her, her eyes darting back and forth trying to take in everything. She'd never been inside an *Englisch haus*, but she didn't have time to explore her surroundings as Ralph pulled her over to where Rachel stood with a group of friends.

"Rachel, look who just arrived?"

Rachel turned and then covered her surprise with a smile of welcome. "Susan! Thanks for coming to my party. Isn't it great?" Rachel leaned over and gave her a hug, catching Susan completely by surprise.

Susan nodded her head, "Happy birthday." She smoothed her hands over her apron, feeling completely out of her element in her Amish dress, apron and prayer *kapp*. "Rachel, you mentioned a dress?" she asked hesitantly, wondering if coming here had been a bad idea.

"I certainly did. Girls, if you'll excuse us for a few minutes?" she told the group of friends she'd been talking with. "Come with me," she grabbed Susan's hand and pulled her up a staircase and down a hallway. She pushed open a door at the end and Susan found herself in a very feminine bedroom.

"I have it right here," Rachel smiled at her, pulling a black garment from the middle of her closet.

Susan looked at the dress and her eyes grew wide, even as she began shaking her head. "Rachel, I couldn't wear something like that."

"Of course you can. With your figure, you'll look great in it," Rachel waved away her protests.

Susan held up the dress, blanching when she realized it was going to come quite a few inches about her knees. It was sleeveless as well, and had a plunging neckline. It was so far from her normal mode of dress, she knew she was going to feel practically naked. *It's what everyone else is wearing downstairs and you want to fit in, don't you?*

"Why don't you slip into the bathroom and put it on and then I'll help you do your makeup." Susan glanced towards the bathroom and then murmured, "I don't wear makeup."

Rachel laughed, "I know that. That's why I'm going to help you do it."

Susan took a breath and then shook her head, "I'll wear the dress, but I don't think I want any makeup."

Rachel regarded her and then shrugged her shoulders, "Whatever. Leave that thing covering your hair up here with your clothing." She walked across the room and grabbed a brush off of her dresser. "Use this to do something with your hair if you want. I'll be downstairs. Come join the party once you're dressed."

Rachel started to leave and then turned back, "Oh, I forgot. You need shoes." She reached into the bottom of her closet and produced a pair of red shoes with spiky heels, "These will be perfect."

Susan took the shoes, "I can't wear these."

"Sure you can. They'll look great with that dress. Just take it slow coming down the stairs. I don't want you breaking your neck before enjoying yourself." She left the bedroom and Susan took the dress and retreated to the bathroom.

The dress was so short! She tugged at the hem, feeling awkward and unsure of herself as she looked at her reflection in the bathroom mirror. The dress was black and tight, and the darts and seams around the bodice served to give her cleavage she hadn't imagined she owned.

She finally convinced herself to leave the bathroom and she sat on the edge of the bed as she slipped the red shoes on her feet. It took her several tries before she could walk across the room without her ankles wobbling and feeling like she was about to fall over. Thirty minutes after being led to Rachel's bedroom, she finally felt confident enough to join the others downstairs.

She'd used the borrow brush on her hair and it now fell in soft waves down her back, almost touching her waist it was so long. She'd not worn her hair down since she'd been a toddler and it felt strange to feel it brushing against the bare skin of her back. She held onto the railing as she made her way down the staircase, biting her lip as guys whistled at her and smiled in appreciation.

Ralph was waiting for her by the time she traversed the staircase, a look of wonder and happiness on his face. "Susan, you look hot!"

She blushed and bit her lip harder, "Thanks."

"Come on, I'll introduce you to some people," Ralph told her, pulling her around the room. Susan didn't even try to remember everyone's name, relegating this to a one-time event and figuring she wouldn't ever need their names again.

"So, what do you think about your first party?" Ralph asked her a little bit later.

"It all feels kind of strange. It was really nice of Rachel to invite me."

Ralph nodded, popping a pretzel into his mouth and chewing before responding. "I was actually surprised, but I'm glad you came."

"Me too…," she blushed at the look in his eyes. She reached for the hem of the dress once again, tugging it downward.

"Quit fidgeting, you look beautiful."

"It's so short…"

"You look fine." Ralph started to say something else, but suddenly the entire *haus* went dark.

A few second later, black lights were turned on, and everyone spent a few minutes looking around at how anything white took on an unearthly glow.

Ralph touched her shoulder, "Be right back, we must have blown a fuse." She felt and heard him step away from her, leaving her standing alone. Susan turned in a circle, feeling the change in the room as a silence descended over it. She was trying to figure out what had captured everyone's attention, when the sound of Rachel's laughter erupted and Susan turned to see her pointing her direction. When she started clapping her hands, Susan looked around, alarmed to see that she had become the center of attention.

Everyone was pointing at her and laughing outright at something. She could hear words being whispered around her, and then she caught sight of her reflection in a mirror across the room. She looked down and gasped to find the word HOMEWRECKER written all over the dress! It glowed like a beacon in the night and she tried to cover the words with her hands, but it was written across both the front and the back of the dress.

She felt tears spring to her eyes as she looked at Rachel, seeing the hatred shining in the other girl's eyes. "Why?" she whispered brokenly amidst the laughter and taunts coming from the other party goers.

Rachel stopped clapping and advanced on her, causing Susan to back up until she could go no further. "Because you've been trying to steal Ralph from me since the day you met him. All he can talk about it you and the Amish. It makes me sick! We were very happy before you came along!"

Susan shook her head, embarrassment making any sort of speech impossible. She pushed past Rachel, her only goal to reach the front doors and escape these people. Her tears were blinding, but she still managed to find her way to the edge of town and the dirt paths that would take her home. She'd abandoned the awful red high heels in the grass outside Rachel's front door, and her feet were sore from stepping on sharp stones along the way.

Her face felt hot, and she still wore the hateful dress, but she'd wanted to escape so badly, she'd not even given a thought to changing back into her own clothing. She made her way towards the back of her parents' *haus*, her sobs loud enough she feared she would wake her parents up. A fear that was realized as she stepped inside the kitchen.

Two weeks later...

Susan arrived at the orphanage, having taken two weeks off. The thought of seeing anyone who'd been at Rachel's party had caused her to hide amongst her own. She'd arrived home the night of the party, broken, sobbing uncontrollably, and unable to keep from waking up her parents as she tried to sneak back into her bedroom.

They had stared at her in shock and disappointment when they'd seen how she was dressed. And that was without seeing the ugly words that were written all over it.

"Susan? What is the meaning of this? Why are you dressed like...like..."

Her *daed* hadn't even been able to come up with the words to describe how she was attired. Her feet had been covered in small cuts from rushing home barefoot, her hair was a tangled mess around her shoulders, dirt was smeared on her legs and hands from where she'd fallen several times, and a small scrape on her cheek oozed blood from where a branch had been in her way.

Her *mamm* had looked at her with sad eyes, but then heated some water and quietly helped bathe her feet and other injuries. Susan had cried the entire time, knowing she didn't deserve such treatment. Her *daed* had turned his back on her and gone back upstairs to his bed. She'd felt so guilty….

"*Mamm*, do you hate me?" she'd asked through her tears.

The woman who'd raised her had given her a hug and then shaken her head, "*Nee*. Disappointed, but I still love you. As does you *daed*." She was quiet for a moment and then had suggested Susan put her own nightclothes on and try to get some rest. In the morning, she could explain to them what had occurred.

That had been two weeks ago. Two weeks where she'd tried to forget the humiliation she'd felt and how she'd abused the trust her parents had placed in her. They agreed to keep her transgressions just between them, not wanting to damage her reputation within the *Ordnung*. As her *daed* had explained it to her, she'd made a foolish mistake. She'd learned her lesson, one they'd tried to instill in her for years. The *Englisch* were evil and not to be trusted.

Susan had struggled over the last two weeks trying to reconcile what she knew about Ralph and Mrs. Templeton, with the actions of Rachel. They were all *Englisch*, and yet their behaviors so different.

"Susan? I wondered what had happened to you. Ralph said there had been an incident involving his ex-girlfriend."

Ex-girlfriend? "I apologize for not letting you know I wouldn't be here…"

"No need to apologize. Are you okay, dear?" Mrs. Templeton asked her.

Susan nodded slowly, "*Ja*. I will be fine. Is it okay if I go back and see the *kinner?*" She had a strong desire to see the little ones that had come to mean so much to her. When Mrs. Templeton nodded her head, she headed down the hallway.

She walked past the room where Ralph normally volunteered, and was unable to stop herself from glancing into the room to see if he was there today. She couldn't decide if she was relieved or saddened to see a female volunteer reading to the children. Swallowing, she walked to the next room and stepped inside, tears springing to her eyes when Amber and Peter both rushed across the room and threw themselves against her legs.

"You came back!"

"We thought you forgot about us!"

Susan squatted down and hugged them and the other *kinner* close, "I could never forget you. I missed you."

"We missed you too. Kate's gots a new home!" Amber told her excitedly.

"She did?"

"Uh huh. Mrs. Templeton said they were going to adopt her. Does that mean she won't have to come back here again?"

Susan smiled, "That's exactly what it means." She looked around the room and then suggested, "How about we go outside and play for a while?"

"Yay!" came a chorus of happy voices.

Susan escorted them outside and sat on a bench while they played on the swings and slides. She'd been forced to tell her parents about volunteering at the orphanage when she'd explained how she'd come to meet Rachel. As she'd expected, they had asked her to stop going. For her own sake.

Her *daed* had left the decision up to her, and Susan had spent many evenings after dinner talking with *Gott* as she walked in the nearby fields. She'd asked for His divine wisdom in regards to volunteering at the orphanage, and after several days and nights, she'd finally felt the peace she'd been looking for. *Gott* wanted her to spend time with the *kinner* at the orphanage.

She'd explained her decision to her parents and been surprised when they'd nodded their heads and asked her to be more cautious in the future. She'd promised she would be. They knew where she was, and that took an immense weight off of her shoulders.

At the end of her shift, she stopped by Mrs. Templeton's office and knocked lightly on the door. "Come in."

"Sorry to bother you, but I'm getting ready to leave and was wondering why Ralph wasn't here today?"

Mrs. Templeton smiled, "Oh, I'm sorry Susan. He hasn't been here for a few weeks either. I believe he's gone back to school. He was trying to decide if he wanted to attend graduate school or not, and I guess he must have made his decision."

"Oh." Susan digested that bit of information and bid her a good day, "See you next week."

"Next week it is."

Susan slowly made her way home, trying to keep her heart from hurting. *Ralph's gone and I didn't even get a chance to tell him goodbye.*

She wandered down to the small pond behind the barn, sitting down next to the large oak tree and watching the ducks move effortlessly across the water's surface.

Gott, I don't understand. I tried to protect my heart from becoming attached to him because he was Englisch, and yet, it now feels broken. I'm twenty-two and I want a familye and haus of my own. But I also want Your will in my life.

She cried for herself and for the dreams she'd allowed to fill her mind that would never come to fruition. She knew *Gott* had someone special for her, she now had to patiently wait. And pray for more faith.

Beginning of September…

Susan had just finished peeling potatoes for the casserole she and her *mamm* were making for their dinner when her *daed* came through the back door, "There's an *Englischer* standing in the front yard."

Susan looked up at him, "An *Englischer?*"

"*Ja.*"

"Did you speak to him? Or he to you?"

Her *daed* shook his head, "*Nee.* He's just standing there watching the *haus.*"

Her *mamm* didn't like that at all and started for the front door, only to be pulled back. "I think Susan should deal with this. Come take a walk with me."

Susan was puzzled, but she headed for the front door, curious as to why there was an *Englischer* here. She glanced out the side window and then gasped. The *Englischer* was Ralph!

She opened the door and stepped out onto the porch, wiping her hands nervously on her apron. She didn't speak to him, she just watched him for several long moments before he stepped towards her.

"Susan?"

"Hi. What are you doing here?"

"I had to come see you."

Susan watched him as he slowly stepped up onto the porch, "I thought you went back to school?"

Ralph nodded, "I did. For a few weeks, but I decided that wasn't where I wanted, or needed, to be."

Susan said nothing for a while, she simply turned and sat down on one of the wooden rockers that sat there. Ralph joined her, watching her carefully before speaking again.

"I'm so sorry for what happened at Rachel's party. I had no idea she could be so cruel…" He shook his head and then looked at her with tears shining in his eyes, "I broke up with her. She didn't understand why I was upset…I can't believe I ever saw anything good in her."

"She's a very unkind person," Susan agreed. In her heart, she'd already forgiven Rachel for her cruelty, "I pray that one day she will find *Gott* and be at peace."

Ralph gave her an incredulous look, "You pray for her? But she tried to humiliate you?"

"She succeeded, but only for a short while. I trusted in the wrong person, and I wasn't true to myself. I knew I didn't belong in the *Englisch* world…your world."

"I don't know that I want to be part of my world," Ralph told her, causing her to look at him with a question in her eyes. He nodded, "Since meeting you and learning more about the way the Amish live, I can't stop thinking about how peaceful your lives must be. I've tried to find happiness and peace all of my life, but in the end, there's always chaos and heartache."

Susan said nothing, she just listened as he spoke from his heart. "You are such a kind and compassionate person, and you make me want to be a better person. A better man." He paused and then asked, "Would you ever consider going on a date with me?"

"Ralph…I'm Amish. If I've learned one thing from all of this, it is that I belong in this world. I like it here and I believe I'm in *Gott's* will here."

He nodded his head and then asked, "So the answer is no?"

Susan nodded her head, even though she wanted nothing more than to tell him yes. She'd thought she'd dealt with her budding feelings for this *mann*, but that wasn't the case at all.

"What if I learned more about your lifestyle and became Amish? Would you go on a date with me then? I have to tell you, I think I'm falling in love with you."

She looked up at him, "What?"

Ralph nodded, "I'm serious. I've missed you and I want to know everything there is to know about you. I want to know this *Gott* you talk about and to. I feel like there's something missing in my life. I want to take a step back and start concentrating on the things that really matter. I want to get married and have kids…"

"*Kinner.*"

"*Kinner.* I want to have some *kinner*, but I don't want to see them grow up in a world where humiliating another human being is seen as fun. Where stepping on people to get the next promotion is encouraged." He stopped and looked at her, "How would I do that?"

"Become Amish?" she questioned, scared to think that he might be serious. If Ralph were to become Amish, the feelings they had for one another would no longer be wrong. And if his feelings for her were real, they could potentially have a future together. But most *Englisch* who tried to convert to the Amish way of life only lasted a few weeks or months. And until he had proven himself, she needed to protect her heart as much as possible.

"You would have to speak with the elders and gain their support. They would then find you a place to live and a job to work at during a probationary period. You be expected to learn to speak and read German, and if you decided to become baptized into the Amish lifestyle, you would have to leave everything else behind."

"So, all or nothing, huh?"

Susan nodded her head, "*Ja.* All or nothing. This is our life, not a game." She didn't mean to sound harsh or pessimistic, but he had asked and what he was suggesting was nearly impossible for most people.

"Can you introduce me to these elders?"

Susan shook her head, turning as booted feet sounded on the porch. She smiled, "*Nee,* I can't, but if you can convince my *daed* you're serious, he could make those introductions." She introduced the two and then left them sitting on the porch. Ralph had just told her he was in love with her and wanted to become Amish, and her head was reeling.

She headed towards the pond, talking to *Gott* as she walked, "He's here. I can't believe it. And he said he's falling in love with me and broke up with Rachel. I didn't tell him I love him back. Not yet. I don't want to get my hopes up and have then broken if he can't leave his *Englisch* upbringing behind him."

Six weeks later…

A knock sounded on the front door and Susan watched as her *daed* answered it. A moment later, Ralph stepped into the room, greeting her *mamm* and herself. "I thought maybe you would like to go for a walk?"

Susan looked at her *daed*, breaking into a smile when he nodded his head in approval, "*Ja.* A walk would be nice."

She stepped outside and walked side by side with him towards the pond. It seemed to be the place she most often came when needing answers, and tonight was no different. "How is working in the furniture shop?"

"*Gut. Wunderbaar.* I am learning much."

"*Gut.*" She stopped and then asked him, "Why are you here?"

Ralph reached for her hand, brushing the back of her knuckles with his fingertips, "I'm here to tell you that I've decided to become baptized. It will take place in three weeks' time."

Susan smiled at him, "Congratulations."

"*Danke.*" He turned her hand over and traced the lines in her palm, watching her as shiver rushed across her shoulders, "I want to court you. I know it's too soon to talk marriage yet, but I love you and want to spend the rest of our lives together."

Susan's felt her heart burst wide open. "I love you too," she murmured to him softly. "I have for a long time, even when you were still with Rachel. I felt so guilty for that…"

"I couldn't see what was right in front of me. Can I court you for a while, and if everything works out, then can we set a date for a wedding?"

"What is a while?" she asked, teasing him softly.

"A week?" he suggested with a smirk.

"*Nee.* That's not nearly long enough. How about a year?"

"Too long. Two weeks."

"Four."

"Three, and that's my final answer. Three weeks from tomorrow we will be married. I've even found us a place to live and some land to buy. I have a fund left to me by my grandfather. I've already spoken to the elders and asked if I could use that money to purchase land and a home for myself and was given a green light."

Susan was overjoyed at hearing his news and before she really thought about it, she turned into his arms and hugged him close. "*Danke.* For coming back for me. When I heard you'd gone back to school, I'd almost given up hope. But then you were standing on the front, like an answer to my prayers."

Ralph hugged her close and then kissed her forehead, "There's still so much I'm unsure of, but you'll help me, wont' you?"

Susan nodded and leaned her head against his shoulder, "*Ja.* I will help you and together, we will do much."

As they headed back to the *haus*, Susan gave silent thanks to *Gott* for bringing about the completion of her dreams. Ralph was proof that *Gott* did care for her and if she simply kept her faith, He would be faithful in keeping His promises to them. Something would strive to never forget again.

By signing up to Hannah Schrock's mailing list you will be the very first to hear about all of her new releases. Members of her mailing list always get the lowest possible price on new books PLUS you will also get occasional FREE Amish stories.

Click Here to add your email address!

I would like to thank you for taking the time to download my book. I really hope that you enjoyed it as much as I enjoyed writing it.

If you feel able I would love for you to give the book a short review on Amazon.

If you want to keep up to date with all of my latest releases then please like my FACEBOOK PAGE

Many thanks once again, all my love.

Hannah.

LATEST BOOKS

DON'T MISS HANNAH'S BRAND NEW MAMMOTH AMISH

MEGA BOOK - 20 Stories in one box set.

Mammoth Amish Romance Mega Book 20 books in one set

Outstanding value for 20 books

OTHER BOX SETS

Amish Romance Mega book (contains many of Hannah's older titles)
Amish Love and Romance Collection

MOST RECENT SINGLE TITLES

The Mysterious Amish Suicide
The Pregnant Amish Quilt Maker
The Amish Caregiver
The Amish Detective: The King Family Arsonist
The Amish Gift
Becoming Amish
The Amish Foundling Girl
The Heartbroken Amish Girl
The Missing Amish Girl
Amish Joy
The Amish Detective
Amish Double
The Burnt Amish Girl

AMISH ROMANCE SERIES

AMISH HEARTACHE

AMISH REFLECTIONS: AMISH ANTHOLOGY COLLECTION

MORE AMISH REFLECTIONS : ANOTHER AMISH ANTHOLOGY COLLECTION

THE AMISH WIDOW AND THE PREACHER'S SON

AN AMISH CHRISTMAS WITH THE BONTRAGER SISTERS

A BIG BEAUTIFUL AMISH COURTSHIP

AMISH YOUNG SPRING LOVE BOX SET

AMISH PARABLES SERIES BOX SET

AMISH HEART SHORT STORY COLLECTION

AMISH HOLDUP

AN AMISH TRILOGY BOX SET

AMISH ANGUISH

SHORT AMISH ROMANCE STORIES

AMISH YOUNG SPRING LOVE SHORT STORIES SERIES

AMISH REJECTION

AMISH BETRAYAL

THE AMISH BONTRAGER SISTERS SHORT STORIES SERIES

AMISH RETURN

AMISH BONTRAGER SISTERS COMPLETE COLLECTION

AMISH APOLOGY

AMISH UNITY

AMISH DOUBT

AMISH FAMILY

THE ENGLISCHER'S GIFT

AMISH SECRET

AMISH PAIN

THE AMISH PARABLES SERIES

THE AMISH BUILDER

THE AMISH PRODIGAL SON

AMISH PERSISTENCE

THE AMISH GOOD SAMARITAN

Also Out Now:

The Mysterious Amish Suicide

Leah Kauffman is distraught when she learns of her beloved brother's death. It all seems like a terrible nightmare, which only gets worse when the police confirm it was suicide after pulling Levi's body from the storm-swollen river.

The Amish community rallies together to support Leah and her father in their time of grief, but Leah can't accept such a simple explanation. She knew her brother better than anyone, and she refuses to believe that he would have thrown away the precious gift of life. With the help of her lifelong best friend, Jonah, Leah embarks on a mission to uncover the truth about her brother's untimely death.

Was Levi really so distraught over the impending marriage of his true love to another man, or were far more sinister forces at work? Along the way, she uncovers truths she never would have imagined - including truths about herself and her relationship with Jonah.

Here is a Taster:

Leah had to remind herself to breathe. A pressure filled her chest, as though something sat on it. She could hardly think, move, do anything without a great deal of willpower. It was an effort to stay upright. She wanted to lie on her bed and cry her eyes out.

Sometimes she felt dizzy, her head spinning. It made her think of the games she'd play with Levi when they were small. They would see how far they could walk in a straight line after spinning around in circles, giggling together as they stumbled around and fell.

She was still dizzy, only she was without Levi. She had never been without him. He'd been her one constant since she was born. He was gone.

The police officers shifted in place before her, which gave her a view of the wall behind them, and the clock there. Was it that late already? No wonder she felt dizzy and weak—she hadn't eaten in hours.

Rain beat on the roof, pouring down in front of the windows in a torrent. It had been raining hard since not long after Jonah reached her at the farmer's market to tell her the news about Levi. As though the heavens opened up to cry the tears she worked so hard to contain.

It didn't seem real, and not just because it had only been a handful of hours since Jonah gave her the news of her brother's disappearance. It would never seem real, no matter how much time passed. Her brother, jumping into the river.

She glanced over at Amos, who sat by the hearth with two other police officers. It was a rare sight, so many Englischer officers in her little kitchen.

Her community stayed away from them as a rule, choosing to solve their problems on their own. The Amish were a self-contained people. This was far too big a problem to keep to themselves, however, and Leah preferred the police become involved if it meant finding her brother's body and finding out what really happened to him. She would never believe he jumped of his own free will.

Amos said he did, however. She listened to what he told the officers, the same story he'd been telling for hours. "We were on an errand for my father, inquiring about a new shipment of wood. I noticed Levi seemed melancholy, though he wouldn't share his feelings with me. I noted how unusual it was for him to behave that way, since he didn't normally. Whenever I spoke to him, I had to repeat myself to be heard. He wasn't paying attention—he was too troubled, too distracted. We stopped to talk with a few of my father's customers who asked about work they waited on. Levi slipped away when I didn't notice."

One of the officers cleared his throat. "What made you think to look for him by the river?"

"I passed the river along my route," he explained. "I finished walking to the mill, then turned back. I saw him on the bridge not far from the mill, along the river. Nobody ever goes there—it's in disrepair and half-concealed by high grass. I called out to him, but it was as if he didn't hear me. At first, I thought he was only looking into the water, thinking. He looked just as sad as he had before. I began to walk toward him, but he jumped into the water before I could reach him."

Leah closed her eyes, squeezing them shut against the mental image of her brother leaping into the river. What could have inspired him to do something like that? It made no sense. It went against everything she knew to be true about her brother, who she'd always thought she knew better than anybody in the world—better even than her best friend, Jonah.

Jonah stood in a corner of the room, away from the conversation. He was always there, though, always the single calming presence she relied on. Just as he'd been for her entire life—so steady, strong, reliable. She needed him more than ever.

His eyes met hers, and she saw the sadness and sympathy in them. There was nothing he could say to make her feel better, but just his presence gave her a little extra strength.

She wished he could do the same for her father, who looked completely broken. Almost no one could get through to him. His only son—first his wife, then his son.

"We'll have to wait for the rain to stop, I'm afraid." Leah looked up at the lead officer, who continued to explain himself. "The river is so swollen, our teams can't find much of anything. It shouldn't rain for but another hour or two, according to the forecast."

Only another hour or two. Considering that it felt like a lifetime since Jonah found her, begging her to go home to be with her father after hearing about Levi's jump, it would be another lifetime before the searchers could continue their work.

Leah stood, going to Jonah with eyes full of tears. "How could this be?" she whispered.

"I don't know," he murmured. "We'll never know, I guess."

She looked at him, seeing the pain in her heart reflected in his eyes. He was never as close with Levi as he was with her, but he appeared just as shaken as she felt. It was too unbelievable to be true, and yet there was no denying it. Amos was certain he saw Levi jump, and there was little chance he could have survived the fall. It was clear nobody there had any hope of her brother coming home alive.

An officer walked downstairs, his feet heavy on the wooden boards. In his hand, he held a sheet of folded paper. He'd gone through Levi's room—it was difficult for Leah to sit idly by and allow it to happen, as she felt it was an invasion of her brother's privacy. In her heart, he was still alive. He would walk through the door any minute, soaked to the skin, with a story of slipping from the bridge and being swept downstream. He'd always been a strong swimmer, and he had a way of making even the dreariest experience sound interesting in the telling.

The officer handed the paper to another man, then another. They all skimmed the lines of neat, handwritten script. Leah resisted the urge to tell them to mind their own business. Another invasion.

Jonah must have read the tension in her, for he placed a calming hand on her arm. "Anything that will help them," he murmured. "They must do their job." Leah let out a sigh of defeat. He was right—he usually was, almost always more level-headed than she was. While Leah was quick to action, Jonah sat back to consider all possible outcomes before committing himself one way or another.

Eventually, the paper found its way into Leah's hands. By the light of the oil lamp over the sink, she and Jonah read its contents. A letter from Rachel. Leah gasped softly. "Rachel Troyer?" she murmured.

"Not Troyer for much longer," Jonah observed quietly. "She says she'll be married to another man from her community next month."

Tears filled Leah's eyes. Oh, poor Levi.

She turned to the officers. "Did you find the envelope to this letter?"

One of the nodded, holding it out to her. The postmark bore all the evidence she needed. It was dated the day before, meaning it had to have arrived that morning. It was all too much to make sense of.

"Who was this Rachel Troyer to your brother, Miss Kauffman?" The man had kind eyes and a gentle voice. He wasn't one of the gruff, all-business officers around her. He seemed to genuinely sympathize with her confusion and grief. Just the same, Leah didn't want to go into Levi's past with Rachel for fear of what it implicated.

Jonah's hand once again reassured her, squeezing her arm gently. Yes. It was for the best. She cleared her throat prior to speaking.

"Levi met Rachel at a party three summers ago. She was visiting from Ohio at the time, staying with cousins. Levi...fell in love with her." Leah blushed furiously as her father's sad, empty eyes met hers. She hated talking about Levi's personal life with strangers, or even in front of her father. It hadn't been a secret, Levi's feelings for Rachel, but it felt as though she betrayed him nonetheless.

"Did they have a relationship?" one of the officers asked.

"They wrote all the time, sometimes twice a week, maybe more—whenever Levi could get a little time away. Rachel came back every summer, too.

That was as far as their relationship went. Our lives are not like yours."

The kind officer smiled. "We know that. You don't need to explain. Do you know of any of the other letters around here?"

Leah shook her head in all honesty. "I don't know that he kept them, or where."

He nodded. "From the sound of the letter, Rachel was letting him down. Breaking it off."

Leah glanced at the paper in her hand. "Yes, it looks that way. She's to marry another man, at her father's orders." Brief, shining anger flashed through her. Rachel's father had been the only thing standing between them all along. Were it not for him, Leah knew Rachel would happily have moved to Lancaster to marry Levi.

"So a three-year relationship, ended very suddenly by letter today. A jump from a secluded section of the river." The policemen looked at one another. Leah heard the resigned certainty in their voices. Her shoulders slumped. They thought they had the case solved already, she knew.

"I'm sorry to say this," the kind officer said. He took a step closer to Leah. "We have no reason to believe your brother didn't commit suicide."

Leah clenched her fists, raising her chin in defiance.

"I disagree," she said, her voice ringing strong and clear. All eyes shifted to her.

"Leah, please." Jonah sounded deeply concerned. "Don't do this to yourself." As always, his very presence calmed her—but nothing would make her change her mind.

"Miss, I know it seems unbelievable…"

Leah cut the officer's words off with a flash of her eyes on his. He stood down, a sheepish look on his face. "It seems more than unbelievable, sir. It seems unthinkable. Life is the greatest gift Gott gives us. I know my brother —no matter his grief, he would not throw away a precious gift."

Everyone shifted uncomfortably. "I understand," the kind officer said, looking around at the other police to quiet them. "Please understand, Miss Kauffman, that we need to look at all possibilities when doing our work. We can't rule anything out."

She nodded, staying silent. It was no use arguing—they didn't know Levi. They weren't Amish. They were so used to seeing crime and death, they probably didn't hold human life in the same value people such as she and Jonah did. They were immune to the beauty and wonder of it. There would be no convincing them. They would always see her as a grief-stricken sister who refused to accept the truth. She expected them to pat her on the head and send her on her way.

***

Hours later, the kitchen was quiet and virtually empty once again. Only Jonah remained, sitting at the table with a cup of coffee. Leah sat across from him, and she knew he was waiting for her to speak. She also knew he would give her all the time she needed.

Amos had left long before the police did. He was helpful, concerned, clearly distraught. "I should have stopped him. I should have known." There was no way for him to know, and she told him so—besides, she thought, there was no guarantee Amos hadn't missed something concealed in the tall, thick grass all around the bridge. Such as another person, or someone in the water. It would be just like Levi to jump in to help someone else with no thought for his own safety.

Not long after Amos left, her father went to bed. She'd gone so far as to help him up the stairs, as he didn't look as though he could manage it on his own. He was foggy, lost. It reminded Leah of the terrible early days right after her mother's death. Eight years had passed, and Leah still remembered clearly the pain of those days. In the years since, she'd believed that was the hardest time of her life. The past several hours had served to change her opinion.

"Are you hungry?" she asked Jonah.

"I could eat, though it's nothing you should worry about right now. I can fix something."

She smiled. "Doubtful."

"Are you hungry?" he asked.

"No, but I know I need to eat." She knew all too well, and it was with a rueful smile that she stood to put food together. When she was twelve, she'd had no experience with grief. It had been easy to fall into a habit of refusing food, not sleeping well, putting all her energy into caring for her father and older brother. She'd worked herself into exhaustion, to the point where their doctor had ordered her to bed for three days.

She put out a loaf of bread, cheese, cold meat and leftover pie from the refrigerator—one of the few conveniences their ordered allowed. Despite his hesitation, Jonah dug into the food with vigor. Leah smiled softly as she watched him eat.

She rubbed her eyes, feeling more tired than she could remember feeling since those ugly days after a sudden brain hemorrhage ended her mother's life. She felt all cried out, like there wasn't a tear left in her body…though she knew there would be more time to cry before all was said and done. Levi was still out there somewhere, his body floating along the water or maybe caught up in some reeds along the riverbank. She nearly choked on a mouthful of food at the thought.

She pushed the ugly thought from her mind, reminding herself how strong she needed to be for her father. His health was never strong to begin with, though he did the best he could with the help of assistants at the bakery… and Levi.

"Thank you for being here with me," Leah murmured, staring down at the plate of food she had no desire to eat. She forced herself to take a bite of her sandwich, then another.

"Of course," Jonah replied. His blue eyes were so kind, as always, his voice full of gentleness. She wondered if he was ever anything but gentle, patient, kind.

"You may think it's nothing, but it means a lot to me," she insisted. "I don't know what I would do alone."

"You never have to be alone."

Even in her state of grief, Leah blushed. Jonah had a way of saying things which hinted at a deeper meaning. He didn't always speak that way, but when he did Leah invariably felt a flutter in her stomach.

She sighed. "I can't believe he's gone. There's something inside me which won't let me believe it."

He nodded thoughtfully, and took a long time before speaking. That was his way, always thinking things through. "It's quite a shock. More than that, it seems out of character for him."

"Exactly. He wasn't a depressive person. He didn't go around with a frown on his face. He wasn't always happy—who is? But he wasn't the type to act rashly. He wouldn't have thrown his life away like this."

Jonah shrugged. "Who's to say, though? The letter from Rachel...none of us can say what goes on in a person's heart. None of us knows how we would react in a situation such as that. When we love a person, and know they can never be ours. Not only that, but he knew she would be another man's wife." He shook his head. "I'm not sure how I would feel if that happened to me."

Another flutter in her stomach. Even in the deepest grief, Jonah had a way of reaching her heart.

"He could have talked to me about it. He should have. Why didn't he? We could always talk about things."

"I'm sure he wasn't thinking clearly."

Leah shook her head. "No. I refuse to believe this."

"Leah..."

"I mean it, Jonah. He wasn't a rash person. I knew him—I know him," she corrected. She couldn't wrap her mind around the notion of referring to him in past tense. "I know my brother like I know myself. This isn't something he would do. Something else happened. I don't know what. Either there was somebody in the water who he tried to save, or somebody...pushed him." It sounded silly even to her ears, but she couldn't allow herself to entertain another theory."

Jonah sighed as though he knew better than to try to change her mind.

"I need to find out what really happened," she said, leaning across the table toward him. "I need to. I can't live not knowing."

He regarded her in his usual quiet manner, his eyes going over her face. She stared at him with great intensity, willing him to understand what she meant and felt. Of all people, she had to get him to understand.

And he did, as he always did. "I'll help you in any way I can."

She smiled, glowing from within. Just those few words were enough to give her extra strength.

"What would I do without you?" she asked.

"You'll never need to find out." He smiled, taking her plate and his to the sink, then putting the rest of the food away. She was too tired to argue, and yawned as though to punctuate the thought.

"You need some rest," he observed. "It will be a long few days coming up."

Leah nodded. "I know," she said. "I know all too well."

"I'll be here for whatever you need." He turned to her, leaning against the sink. "I mean it. Whatever you need. I hate to think of you going through this all alone."

She smiled wearily. "I'm not alone. I have Gott, not to mention my father."

"Yes, Gott is always there. I fear you'll be caring more for your father than anything else, though."

Leah nodded, chewing her lip. "I know. I hate to think of it that way, but I know."

"Remember," Jonah said, taking his hat from the hook by the door. "No one expects you to be strong all the time. It's important to take care of yourself, too." He saw himself out, and Leah waved as he left. Normally, she would have shown him to the door, but nothing was normal. She felt rooted to the spot, looking around the empty kitchen, wondering if she would ever feel truly happy again. Nothing would be the same without Levi—her first friend, and the best one she'd ever had aside from Jonah.

There was no use fighting the idea that he wasn't coming back. She knew he was gone, felt it in her heart. He would always be with her in spirit, but she would never hear his laugh again. He would never tease her or go out of his way to make her smile when she had a difficult day.

She took the stairs to the second floor one slow step at a time. It almost felt like too much to ask of herself, the simple act of climbing the stairs. Her body and soul were so tired, aching.

Gott would give her strength, and she said a string of prayers as she rested in bed after changing into her nightdress. There was nothing but silence in the house—her father was either sleeping or, more likely, saying his own prayers. Or grieving. Leah wished there was something she could say to lessen his pain, but knew there was nothing. He'd lost his only son.

After at least an hour with no sleep in sight, Leah got out of bed and tiptoed down the hall. She intended to go to Levi's room—somehow, she thought it might feel less painful there. She might be able to pretend he was still with her.

She was too late. Her father had already fallen asleep there. The door was open, he was fully dressed. As though he'd fallen onto the bed in a fit of grief and cried himself to sleep.

Leah tiptoed away without closing the door. She didn't want him to wake up to find that she'd observed him. What could she do for him? She could get to the bottom of how Levi had met his end, for one. Then came the question of how she would do that.

She knew that whatever methods she'd use, she'd have to do it on her own. It would only deepen her father's grief if he found out.

The Mysterious Amish Suicide

Manufactured by Amazon.ca
Bolton, ON

38443808R00022